Shall We Do That Again?

Hiawyn Oram

Illustrated by Sam Williams

ORCHARD BOOKS

For Murray – S.W.

ORCHARD BOOKS
96 Leonard Street, London EC2A 4XD
Orchard Books Australia
Unit 31/56 O'Riordan Street, Alexandria NSW 2015
ISBN 1 84121 709 3 (hardback)
ISBN 1 84121 110 9 (paperback)
First published in Great Britain in 2001
First paperback publication in 2002
Text © Hiawyn Oram 2001
Illustrations © Sam Williams 2001
The right of Hiawyn Oram to be identified as the author and
Sam Williams to be identified as the illustrator
of this work has been asserted by them in accordance
with the Copyright, Designs and Patents Act 1988.
A CIP catalogue record for this book is available from the British Library.
2 4 6 8 10 9 7 5 3 1 (hardback)
2 4 6 8 10 9 7 5 3 1 (paperback)
Printed in Hong Kong/China

Mrs Brownmouse and Little Brownmouse
were walking in the woods.
Mrs Brownmouse hid behind a tree. . .

and popped out with a loud "BOO!"

Little Brownmouse jumped and laughed and laughed.
"Shall we do that again?" she laughed and laughed.

"Hmm, not now," said Mrs Brownmouse, "because right now it's time to turn round and go back."

So they turned round to go back and just
when Mrs Brownmouse wasn't expecting it. . .

Little Brownmouse hid
amongst the flowers. . .

and popped out with a loud "Boooooo!"

Mrs Brownmouse jumped and Little Brownmouse
laughed and laughed.
"Shall we do THAT again?" she laughed and laughed.

"Hmm, not now," said Mrs Brownmouse, putting Little Brownmouse high on her shoulders, "because right now, it's time to get home for supper."

So off they went home for supper and while
Mrs Brownmouse cooked, Little Brownmouse watched
and just when Mrs Brownmouse wasn't expecting it. . .

Little Brownmouse crept
across the room and hid
behind the door. . .

and jumped out with a loud "Baaaah!"

And Mrs Brownmouse waved her wooden spoon
and went "Baaaah!" straight back which sent
Little Brownmouse running under the table,
laughing and laughing.

"Shall we do THAT again?" she laughed and laughed.
"Not right now," said Mrs Brownmouse, "because right
now it's time to eat!"

So they sat down to eat and Little Brownmouse played with her food and Mrs Brownmouse ate her food. . .

and just as she was taking a rather large
mouthful Little Brownmouse slid
down behind her chair. . .

and popped out with a loud "Whaaaaaaao!"

Mrs Brownmouse jumped and ran after her crying,
"What's a little ghost doing in my kitchen?"
And Little Brownmouse laughed and laughed.
"Shall we do THAT again?" she laughed and laughed.

"Not right now," said Mrs Brownmouse,
"because right now it's time for your bath."

So hand in hand, Mrs Brownmouse and
Little Brownmouse went upstairs. . .

and Mrs Brownmouse prepared Little Brownmouse's bath. . .

and Little Brownmouse got into it. . .

and Mrs Brownmouse lathered up the sponge
and got down to the washing, and just when
she wasn't expecting it. . .

Little Brownmouse made a big splash and soaked her!
Mrs Brownmouse shrieked and splashed her back and
Little Brownmouse laughed and laughed.

Splash!

"Shall we do THAT again?" she laughed and laughed. "Hmm, not now," said Mrs Brownmouse, "because right now it's time for your bed!"

So Mrs Brownmouse dried
Little Brownmouse dry. . .

and powdered her. . .

and took hold of her
toes and tickled her
under one. . .

 and tickled her
under two. . .

and tickled her
under three. . .

 and tickled her
under four. . .

and tickled her all the way up. . .
"Wiggly, wiggly, wiggly, wiggly"

from her tubby little toes to her chubby little chin. . .

and Little Brownmouse laughed and laughed and laughed.
"Can we do THAT again?" she laughed and laughed. "PLEASE!"

"Not now," said Mrs Brownmouse. "because right now it's time for your bedtime story."

So Little Brownmouse snuggled down
under her duvet and, after all the excitement,
Mrs Brownmouse read her a quiet bedtime story.
And when it was finished. . .

Little Brownmouse gave Mrs Brownmouse a big hug
and as Mrs Brownmouse was giving her a big hug back. . .

up the stairs crept
Mr Brownmouse. . .

"Boo!" cried Little Brownmouse.
"Boo!"
laughed Mr Brownmouse.

"Shall we do that again?" he laughed
and laughed.
    "Oh, no! Not now!" said Little Brownmouse,
"Because now it's time for. . .

another hug!"